A Note to Parents and Caregivers:

Read-it! Joke Books are for children who are moving ahead on the amazing road to reading. These fun books support the acquisition and extension of reading skills as well as a love of books.

Published by the same company that produces *Read-it!* Readers, these books introduce the question/answer and dialogue patterns that help children expand their thinking about language structure and book formats.

When sharing joke books with a child, read in short stretches. Pause often to talk about the meaning of the jokes. The question/answer and dialogue formats work well for this purpose and provide an opportunity to talk about the language and meaning of the jokes. Have the child turn the pages and point to the pictures and familiar words. When you read the jokes, have fun creating the voices of characters or emphasizing some important words. Be sure to reread favorite jokes.

There is no right or wrong way to share books with children. Find time to read with your child, and pass on the legacy of literacy.

Adria F. Klein, Ph.D.
Professor Emeritus
California State University
San Bernardino, California

Editor: Christianne Jones
Designer: Joe Anderson
Creative Director: Keith Griffin
Editorial Director: Carol Jones
Managing Editor: Catherine Neitge
Page Production: Picture Window Books
The illustrations in this book were created digitally.

Picture Window Books
5115 Excelsior Boulevard
Suite 232
Minneapolis, MN 55416
877-845-8392
www.picturewindowbooks.com

Printed in the United States of America.

Library of Congress Cataloging-in-Publication Data
Ziegler, Mark, 1954-
What's up, doc? : a book of doctor jokes / by Mark Ziegler ; illustrated by
Ryan Haugen.
p. cm. — (Read-it! joke books—supercharged!)
ISBN 1-4048-1165-6 (hardcover)
1. Medicine—Juvenile humor. 2. Physicians—Juvenile humor. I. Haugen,
Ryan, 1972- II. Title. III. Series.

PN6231.M4Z44 2006
818'.602—dc22
                                                      2005004073

What's Up, DOC?

A Book of Doctor Jokes

by Mark Ziegler   illustrated by Ryan Haugen

Special thanks to our advisers for their expertise:

Adria F. Klein, Ph.D.
Professor Emeritus, California State University
San Bernardino, California

Susan Kesselring, M.A.
Literacy Educator
Rosemount–Apple Valley–Eagan (Minnesota) School District

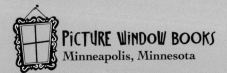

PICTURE WINDOW BOOKS
Minneapolis, Minnesota

Patient: "Doctor, my brother thinks he's invisible!"

Doctor: "Tell him I can't see him now."

Patient: "Doctor, I feel like a piano."

Doctor: "Well, let me make a few notes."

Patient: "Doctor, I feel like a window."

Doctor: "Where's the 'pane'?"

Patient: "Doctor, I feel run down."

Doctor: "Be more careful crossing the street!"

Patient: "Doctor, can you help me? I'm a burglar."

Doctor: "Have you taken anything for it?"

Patient: "Doctor, will this lotion clear up the red spots on my arm?"

Doctor: "I never make rash promises."

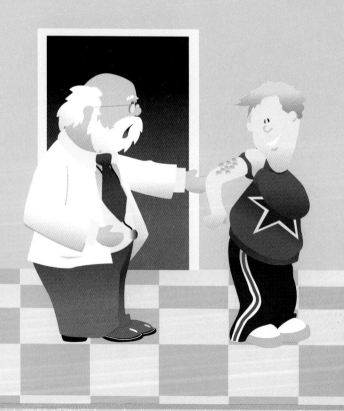

Patient: "Doctor, can you help me out?"

Doctor: "Yes, which way did you come in?"

Patient: "Doctor, can I have a second opinion?"

Doctor: "Sure, come back tomorrow."

Patient: "Doctor, I broke my leg in two places!"

Doctor: "Well, don't go back there again!"

Patient: "Doctor, I've got gas."

Doctor: "Good. Go fill up my car."

Patient: *"Doctor, I think I'm a cashew!"*

Doctor: *"You must be nuts!"*

Patient: *"Doctor, everyone disagrees with me."*

Doctor: *"No, they don't!"*

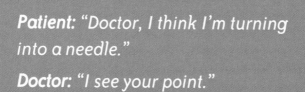

Patient: "Doctor, I think I'm turning into a needle."

Doctor: "I see your point."

Patient: "Doctor, I accidentally swallowed a roll of film!"

Doctor: "Interesting. Let's see what develops."

Patient: *"Doctor, I have this feeling I'm getting smaller and smaller."*

Doctor: *"Don't worry, you'll just have to be a little patient."*

X-ray Lab

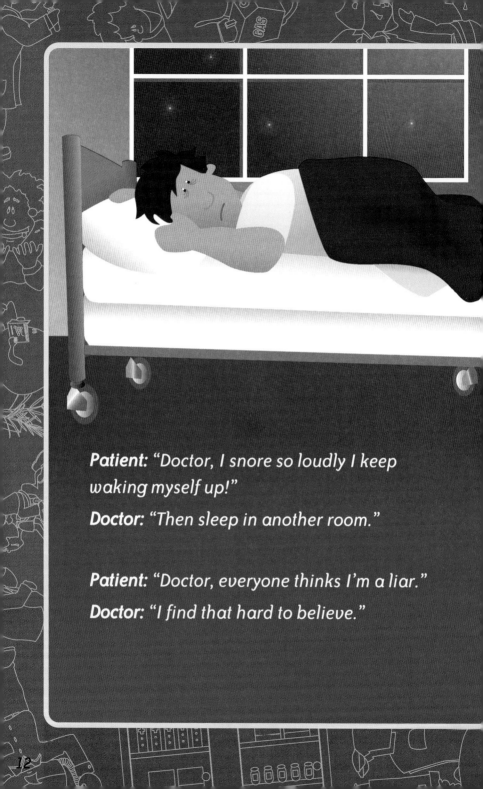

Patient: "Doctor, I snore so loudly I keep waking myself up!"

Doctor: "Then sleep in another room."

Patient: "Doctor, everyone thinks I'm a liar."

Doctor: "I find that hard to believe."

Patient: "Doctor, I think I'm losing my memory!"
Doctor: "When did this happen?"
Patient: "When did what happen?"

Patient: "Doctor, I feel like a pair of curtains!"
Doctor: "Well, pull yourself together!"

Patient: "Doctor, I feel like two different people."

Doctor: "I'll see you one at a time."

Patient: "Doctor, I feel like a rubber band."

Doctor: "I think you're stretching things."

Patient: *"Doctor, I keep seeing a big fly buzzing around my head."*

Doctor: *"It's just a bug going around."*

Patient: *"Doctor, my father keeps acting like a goat!"*
Doctor: *"How long has he been this way?"*
Patient: *"Ever since he was a kid."*

Patient: "Doctor, my mom thinks she's a deck of cards."

Doctor: "I'll deal with her later."

Patient: "Doctor, I feel like a bridge! What's come over me?"

Doctor: "Two cars, a truck, and a motorcycle."

Patient: "Doctor, what did the X-ray of my head show?"

Doctor: "Absolutely nothing."

Patient: "Doctor, I think I'm a sheep."

Doctor: "That's baaaaaaaaaad."

Patient: *"Doctor, I keep hearing a ringing in my ears."*

Doctor: *"Then answer the phone!"*

Patient: *"Doctor, will I need to have shots?"*

Doctor: *"Just one. My aim is pretty good."*

Patient: "Doctor, my sister thinks she's a pony!"

Doctor: "Yes, she does sound a little 'horse.'"

Patient: "Doctor, my little brother fell down the stairs!"

Doctor: "Don't worry, I'll get to the bottom of it."

Patient: "Doctor, I feel like a blueberry!"

Doctor: "Sounds like you're in a jam."

Nurse: "Doctor, are you finished operating on this patient?"

Doctor: "Yes, I've had quite enough out of him!"

Patient: *"Doctor, I feel flushed!"*

Doctor: *"Then don't sit on the toilet!"*

Patient: *"Doctor, I think I have too much iron in my diet."*

Doctor: *"Then stop chewing your nails."*

Patient: "Doctor, I feel like a hamburger."

Doctor: "So do I. Order two of them."

Patient: "Doctor, I think I'm a mummy!"

Doctor: "Stop being so wrapped up in yourself!"

Patient: *"Doctor, my sister swallowed a spoon!"*

Doctor: *"Tell her to sit still and not stir."*

Patient: *"Doctor, sometimes my nose swells up like a doorknob."*

Doctor: *"You need to get a grip!"*

Read-it! Joke Books— Supercharged!

Beastly Laughs: A Book of Monster Jokes by Michael Dahl

Chalkboard Chuckles: A Book of Classroom Jokes by Mark Moore

Chitchat Chuckles: A Book of Funny Talk by Mark Ziegler

Creepy Crawlers: A Book of Bug Jokes by Mark Moore

Critter Jitters: A Book of Animal Jokes by Mark Ziegler

Fur, Feathers, and Fun! A Book of Animal Jokes by Mark Ziegler

Giggle Bubbles: A Book of Underwater Jokes by Mark Ziegler

Goofballs! A Book of Sports Jokes by Mark Ziegler

Lunchbox Laughs: A Book of Food Jokes by Mark Ziegler

Mind Knots: A Book of Riddles by Mark Ziegler

Nutty Names: A Book of Name Jokes by Mark Ziegler

Roaring with Laughter: A Book of Animal Jokes by Michael Dahl

School Kidders: A Book of School Jokes by Mark Ziegler

Sit! Stay! Laugh! A Book of Pet Jokes by Michael Dahl

Spooky Sillies: A Book of Ghost Jokes by Mark Moore

Wacky Wheelies: A Book of Transportation Jokes by Mark Ziegler

Wacky Workers: A Book of Job Jokes by Mark Ziegler

Looking for a specific title or level? A complete list
of *Read-it!* Readers is available on our Web site:
www.picturewindowbooks.com